Peppa Pig

and the

Backyard Circus

This book is based on the TV series *Peppa Pig*.
Peppa Pig is created by Neville Astley and Mark Baker.
Peppa Pig © Astley Baker Davies Ltd/Entertainment One UK Ltd 2003.
www.peppapig.com

First edition 2017

Library of Congress Catalog Card Number pending
ISBN 978-0-7636-9437-1

16 17 18 19 20 21 APS 10 9 8 7 6 5 4 3 2 1

Printed in Humen, Dongguan, China

MIX
Paper from
responsible sources
FSC
www.fsc.org   FSC® C101537

This book was typeset in Peppa.
The illustrations were created digitally.

Candlewick Entertainment
an imprint of Candlewick Press
99 Dover Street
Somerville, Massachusetts 02144

visit us at www.candlewick.com

Peppa Pig and the Backyard Circus

CANDLEWICK
ENTERTAINMENT

It's a sunny day, and Peppa and her friends
are visiting Grandpa and Granny Pig.
Grandpa Pig is using his hammer.

"It's a circus tent!" says Peppa.
"Hooray!" everyone shouts.

"Ooh," says Peppa.
"Can we see
the circus,
Grandpa Pig?"

"This isn't a circus tent," says Grandpa Pig.
"It looks like a circus tent," says Peppa. "What is it?"
"It's for Granny Pig's garden party," he says.
Peppa doesn't know what a garden party is.

Grandpa Pig tells her it's a party where
grown-ups stand around and talk.

It doesn't sound like fun to Peppa.
She has a better idea.

"Let's put on our own show!" says Peppa.
"We'll call it Peppa's Circus."

Granny Pig thinks having
the circus at her garden party
is a very good idea.

Everyone wants to join the circus.
Danny Dog wants to be the strong man.

Emily Elephant wants to be the juggler.

"My father used to work in a circus," says Emily Elephant.

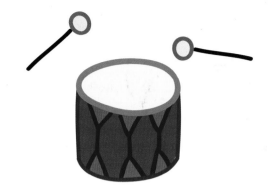

"He did?" asks Peppa. "What did he do?"

Peppa knows that sometimes
there are elephants in the circus.

"He was the ticket taker," says Emily.

Granny Pig brings the dress-up box.
There are lots of fun things inside.

Danny Dog finds polka-dot shorts and a stick-on mustache.
"My strong-man suit!" he says.

Peppa finds a hat.

Pedro Pony finds a clown costume
and a horn.

HONK,
HONK!

Rebecca Rabbit does makeup.

"Hold still, Pedro!" she says.

Everyone is dressed
and ready for the show.

"Grandpa," says Peppa,
"I don't have anything to do."

"Well, you can be the ringmaster," he says.
"What does the ringmaster do?" asks Peppa.
"The ringmaster is the boss," says Grandpa Pig.

Peppa likes that idea. "I will be the ringmaster boss!" she says.
"Good," says Grandpa.

"You can say 'Welcome to my circus. Come and see the amazing feats of derring-do!'"

Granny's guests start to arrive.
Everyone crowds inside the striped tent.

"Welcome to my circus!" shouts Peppa.

"Come and see the amazing feet!"

The circus begins.

"Prepare to be scared," Peppa says.

"Is it a tiger?" Rebecca asks.

"No—it's Candy Cat!"

"Now watch the amazing cyclists—

Squeak!

Squeak!

George, Richard, and Edmond!"

"Here's the strong man, Danny Dog!"

Danny shows his muscles.

He wants to show the crowd how strong he is.

He lifts Peppa!

"Ooooh!" says the crowd.

"Now please welcome Emily Elephant,
who will juggle two potatoes and one egg!"

Toss—drop.
Toss—drop.
Toss—

SPLAT!

When Pedro the clown walks into the ring, everyone laughs.

SPRAY!

HA HA HA!

Everyone laughs again.

"Ladies and gentlemen,
boys and girls,
dogs and elephants,
cats and ponies,"
says Peppa.

"Thank you for coming

to my circus!"

PEACHTREE CITY LIBRARY
201 Willowbend Road
Peachtree City, GA 30269-1623
Phone: 770-631-2520
Fax: 770-631-2522